MW00881008

Copyright © 2019 by Laura Jaworski

Illustration Copyright © 2019 by Laura Jaworski

All rights reserved. No part of this publication may be reproduced, distributed, or transmitted in any form or by any means, including photocopying, recording, or other electronic or mechanical methods, without the prior written permission of the author and illustrator.

Printed in the United States of America

First Printing, 2019

ISBN 9781076976086

www.laurajaworski.com

♡

The Little Tree

by Laura Jaworski

One bright spring morning, a little sapling popped his head up from the ground.

"Hello!" said the sapling.

"Well, hello!" said a nearby willow.

The little sapling began to wiggle all around.

"Whatever are you doing?" asked the willow.

"I don't have my branches yet," said the sapling. "I am trying to pull them up from the ground."

"You are exactly the size that you are meant to be, and it is a beautiful day. Let's enjoy it together," said the willow.

Still, the sapling wiggled.

A few years passed, and the young tree was growing. One day, as he watched the birds soaring across the sky, he began to flap his leaves.

"Whatever are you doing?" asked the willow.

"I want to fly like the birds," said the tree.

"You are exactly where you are meant to be, and it is a beautiful day. Let's enjoy it together," said the willow.

Still, the young tree flapped.

Seasons passed, and the tree continued to grow. One day, as he watched the bugs marching, he began to stretch his roots.

"Whatever are you doing?" asked the willow.

"I want to walk like the bugs," said the tree.

"You move exactly how you are meant to move, and it is a beautiful day. Let's enjoy it together," said the willow.

Still, the tree stretched.

Many years passed, and the young tree grew into a fine oak. But though he wiggled, and flapped, and stretched, still he was not content. With a great sigh, he slumped his weary shoulders.

"I don't think I shall ever be as tall as I'd like," he said. "I don't think I shall ever fly or walk, either."

"Look at the birds in the sky," said the willow. "They fly because they have wings, and because it is their nature."

The oak watched the birds fly.

"Look at the ants march in a row," said the willow. "They march because they have legs, and because it is their nature."

The oak watched the ants march.

"A tree grows tall from sturdy roots," said the willow. "We provide shelter for the animals and the insects. We offer cool shade and fresh air to all who are in need. That is *our* nature."

The oak tree thought deeply about what the willow said.

He felt the soft breeze blowing through his leaves, and he felt peaceful.

He felt his strong, sturdy roots growing in the ground, and he felt secure.

He felt the squirrels and birds living in his branches, and he felt helpful.

Finally, he stopped wiggling, and flapping, and stretching.

Just then, the oak felt a tiny vibration. He looked down, and up popped a new sapling!

"Good morning!" said the little sapling.

"How very nice to meet you," said the oak.

The tiny sapling, who was only a few inches high, began to shimmy and shake.

"Whatever are you doing?" asked the oak.

"I'm too small!" squeaked the sapling. "I want to be tall, like you!"

The towering oak smiled.

"You are exactly the size that you are meant to be, and it's a beautiful day," he said. "Let's enjoy it together."

The End.

FOR MORE BOOKS AND FUN VISIT
WWW.LAURAJAWORSKI.COM

Made in the USA
Middletown, DE
07 March 2021

34977917R00022